MUSEUM MYSTERIES

Museum Mysteries is published by Stone Arch Books
A Capstone Imprint
1710 Roe Crest Drive
North Mankato, MN 56003
www.capstonepub.com

Text and illustrations © 2015 Stone Arch Books

Library of Congress Cataloging-in-Publication Data
Brezenoff, Steven, author.
   The case of the portrait vandal / by Steve Brezenoff ; illustrated by Lisa K. Weber.
      pages cm. -- (Museum mysteries)
Summary: Somebody is vandalizing exhibits at the Capitol City Museum of American History, and it is up to twelve-year-old Raining Sam and his friends to find the culprit before irreparable damage is done.

ISBN 978-1-4342-9685-6 (library binding) -- ISBN 978-1-4965-0194-3 (ebook)
ISBN 978-1-4342-9689-4 (paperback)

1. Historical museums--Juvenile fiction. 2. Vandalism--Juvenile fiction. 3. Detective and mystery stories. 4. Best friends--Juvenile fiction. [1. Mystery and detective stories. 2. Historical museums--Fiction. 3. Museums--Fiction. 4. Vandalism--Fiction. 5. Best friends--Fiction. 6. Friendship--Fiction. 7. Ojibwa Indians--Fiction. 8. Indians of North America--Great Lakes (North America)--Fiction.] I. Weber, Lisa K., illustrator. II. Title.
PZ7.M47833755 Cap 2015
813.6--dc23   2014026182

Designer: K. Carlson
Editor: A. Deering
Production Specialist: G. Bentdahl

Photo Credits: Shutterstock (vector images, backgrounds, paper textures)
Printed in the United States of America in North Mankato, Minnesota.
082020   003783

The Case of the
PORTRAIT VANDAL

By Steve Brezenoff
Illustrated by Lisa K. Weber

STONE ARCH BOOKS
a capstone imprint

The Articles of Confederation

- Represented the first constitutional agreement between the original thirteen states

- Created unity among the states after the American Revolution

- John Dickinson, a delegate from Delaware, was the primary writer of the document

- Adopted by the Continental Congress on November 15, 1777

- Became effective after being ratified by Maryland (the thirteenth and final state) on March 1, 1781

- Replaced by the current U.S. Constitution on March 4, 1789

ARTICLES

OF

Confederation

AND

Perpetual Union

BETWEEN THE

STATES

OF

New Hampshire, Massachusetts Bay, Rhode Island, and Providence Plantations, Connecticut, New York, New Jersey, Pennsylvania, Delaware, Maryland, Virginia, North Carolina, South Carolina, and Georgia.

WILLIAMSBURG:
Printed by ALEXANDER PURDIE.

Amal Farah

Raining Sam

Wilson Kipper

Clementine Wim

Capitol City Sleuths

Amal Farah
Age: 11
Favorite Museum: Air and Space Museum
Interests: astronomy, space travel, and
building models of space ships

Raining Sam
Age: 12
Favorite Museum: American History Museum
Interests: Ojibwe history, culture, and
traditions, American history – good and bad

Clementine Wim
Age: 13
Favorite Museum: Art Museum
Interests: painting, sculpting with clay, and
anything colorful

Wilson Kipper
Age: 10
Favorite Museum: Natural History Museum
Interests: dinosaurs (especially pterosaurs
and herbivores), and building dinosaur models

TABLE OF

CONTENTS

CHAPTER 1
Graffiti Artist

Twelve-year-old Raining Sam sat in the cafeteria of the Capitol City American History Museum, but he wasn't there to eat. In fact, it was only nine o'clock in the morning. The museum had just opened for the day, and the cafeteria wouldn't start serving lunch till eleven.

Instead, Raining studied the big paperback book sitting on the table in front of him. The words American History in Crossword Puzzles were scrawled across the cover. The book had been a gift from the boy sitting next to him, Raining's ten-year-old friend Wilson Kipper.

"Cool, huh?" Wilson said, pulling his chair a little closer. "My mom got me the same book, but mine is about dinosaurs and pterosaurs and ichthyosaurs instead of American history."

"Of course it is," Raining replied with a grin. Wilson and his mom were both a little obsessed with dinosaurs and the other giant reptiles that lived at the same time. It made sense given that Wilson's mom, Dr. Kipper, worked at the Capitol City Natural History Museum.

"So do you like it?" Wilson asked. "We saw it and figured American history would be perfect for you."

Just as Raining knew about Wilson's dinosaur fascination, Wilson knew about Raining's interest in American history, especially the history of his own people, the Ojibwe. The tribe had been on the continent known as North America a lot longer than some other people.

"I like it a lot," Raining said. "Thank you."

"Do you want to start the puzzles?" Wilson asked.

"I don't have a pencil," said Raining. "And besides, the girls will be here soon. I want to show you all the new flag exhibit upstairs."

"The girls" were Clementine Wim and Amal Farah, the other two members of their group. They were due to meet Raining and Wilson at the museum as they often did. Since all four kids had a parent who worked in the Capitol City network of museums, they took turns visiting the different institutions. Raining's father was the Head of Educational Programs at the American History Museum, which was where they'd decided to meet today.

"Okay," said Wilson. He hopped down from his chair and headed for the door.

"Where are you going?" Raining asked, turning in his seat. "They're not here *yet*."

"Yes, they are," Wilson said. "I can hear their feet on the stairs outside."

Raining strained to listen. He could hear something — probably footsteps — but how could Wilson know who they belonged to?

But sure enough, the cafeteria door swung open a moment later, and Amal and Clementine walked in.

"How'd you do that?" Raining said.

Wilson shrugged. "I can just tell from the way they walk, I guess."

"Amazing," said Raining, standing up from his spot at the table. "And people think *we're* supposed to be the trackers." It bugged Raining that people he met still assumed certain things about North America's indigenous people.

"Hey, guys," Amal said as she walked over. "What's the plan for today?"

"I want to get to the Flag Room first thing," Raining said.

"Works for me," Clementine agreed easily. "Lead the way."

"So, Raining," Amal said, putting an arm around his shoulders as they walked. Amal was a year younger than Raining, but several inches taller, almost as tall as thirteen-year-old Clementine. "Tell me about the Flag Room."

"Well," Raining said, "it's new. It opened last week. My father wanted to add a flag display mostly for the field trips he brings through. Lots of the younger classes do a unit on the history of the flag."

"Makes sense," Amal said.

"And it's got every flag the country has ever used?" Clementine asked him. "Like, with different numbers of stars and all that?"

"Oh, it has way more than that," Raining said. He climbed the big marble staircase to the second floor where the new Flag Room was. "Did you know that the first flag our country used didn't have any stars at all?"

Raining didn't need to go on, because just then, they reached the new Flag Room. The high walls were lined with flags displayed behind protective glass. Each one had its own spotlight and a placard describing the flag and telling what years it had been used.

But Raining was right. The Flag Room had way more than just the old Stars and Stripes on display. There were some flags that, though never officially flags of the United States, had been flown years and years ago unofficially.

On the wall closest to them hung a yellow flag that had a coiled rattlesnake in the middle. Under the snake it said, "Don't tread on me." Another flag next to that was almost all red except for a white field with a green pine tree in the upper left corner.

"What's that?" Clementine asked. "A Christmas flag?"

"Don't be silly," said Wilson. He walked over to it and read the description on the placard. "It says it's the Continental Flag of 1775. It was flown by American forces at the Battle of Bunker Hill. It's based on the flag of New England."

Clementine shrugged. "I'd prefer Christmas," she said, strolling along the length of the wall and looking up at the flags.

"What's this one?" Amal asked, stepping up next to Raining. Together they glanced up at a familiar flag. It looked like the current United States flag, but instead of fifty stars on a blue field, it had a circle of stars.

"That's the original Betsy Ross flag," Raining said. "Each star represents one of the original thirteen English colonies."

Amal squinted up at the flag.

"Don't you trust me?" Raining said. "There are thirteen."

"I'm not counting," she replied, standing on her tiptoes to get a closer look at the circle of stars. "I'm wondering why there's a silly looking smiley face drawn in black marker in the middle of the circle."

"There's what?" Raining said. He squinted up at the flag too. There was something there, but it was hard to tell what it was under the glare of the spotlight. "I can't quite make it out."

Raining hurried over to the entrance to the Flag Room and looked out. Luckily one of the museum's security guards was walking by just then.

"Eddie!" Raining called to the guard. "Is there a ladder I can use?"

Eddie stopped and scratched his head. "A ladder?" he said. He took a step into the Flag Room. "Why do you want a ladder?"

All the guards knew Raining, of course, because of his father's position at the museum. As the Head of Educational Programs, he did a lot of work on getting new exhibits for the museum, and Raining was around a lot. In fact, so were his three best friends.

"Amal spotted something on the Betsy Ross flag," Raining said, walking back to it and pointing up. "I want a closer look."

"Hmm," said Eddie. He opened an unmarked door in the Flag Room and pulled out a short ladder — more like an overgrown stepstool, really — and climbed up. Raining and his friends stood around the ladder and watched the guard.

"I see what you're talking about," Eddie said. He licked his finger and rubbed at the markings. "It won't come off. We'll need to some strong glass cleaner."

"Then it's not on the flag?" Raining said. "Just the frame?"

"Yup," said Eddie. He climbed back down the ladder and grabbed his walkie-talkie from his belt. "You there, Mac? Send someone from maintenance up to the Flag Room, will you? I've got some graffiti on one of the frames."

The security guard replaced his walkie-talkie and turned back to Raining and his friends. "Such a shame," he said. "Who would do something so juvenile?"

"I guess someone who doesn't like the museum," Wilson said.

"Or someone who doesn't like that flag," Clementine suggested.

Amal shrugged. "Or just someone with a black marker and a chip on his shoulder."

Eddie nodded. "Could've been anyone," he said as he carried the ladder back to the closet and put it away. "Well, thanks for letting me know, Raining. It'll be cleaned up before lunchtime."

Eddie left to go back to his patrols, and the four sleuths stood together under the Betsy Ross flag.

Raining stared up at the clearly marred frame. "Are you guys thinking what I'm thinking?" he asked.

The others all nodded.

"There's a vandal in the museum," Wilson said.

"A graffiti artist," Amal added.

Clementine sneered up at the sloppy black ink and shook her head. "And not a very good one."

CHAPTER 2
Another Victim

There was a lot more to the American History Museum than just the new flag exhibit, so the four friends roamed the halls slowly, looking at the portraits and busts of famous Americans and wandering in and out of other exhibit halls.

At first, everything seemed normal.

"Maybe the Betsy Ross flag is the only victim," Wilson said hopefully as they found a bench to rest on in the Hall of Documents.

The Hall of Documents was Raining's least favorite room. Even though he loved learning about history, this room was just a bunch of crinkly old paper in glass cases. The words written on the yellowing pages were probably important, but they were so hard to read it didn't much matter.

"Maybe you're right," said Amal. "Maybe this isn't a crime we have to solve."

"And it really could've been anyone," Clementine pointed out. "The security guard got that ladder out of the closet. The door wasn't even locked. Anyone else could have gotten it out too."

"That's true," said Raining. He sighed and stood up, wandering toward the nearest display case. It held a copy of the Articles of Confederation.

Though Raining had never read them, he knew that the Articles of Confederation had been written by the very first American states. The thirteen founding states had signed them as the country's first constitution — that was how the United States of America had become a country.

After a few years, however, the Articles of Confederation had been tossed because the states had been having too many fights. That's when the U.S. Constitution had been created, and that's what kept the United States of America together today.

Raining glanced down at the Articles in their lighted glass case. Even though he wasn't that familiar with them, he knew for sure they didn't have the word "DORKS" scribbled across them in thick, red marker.

"Um, guys?" Raining called, leaning close to the glass. "Come take a look at this."

The others circled around Raining and the case. When she saw what was written on the document, Clementine gasped and clasped a hand over her open mouth.

"It's not as bad as it looks," Raining said. "It's just a copy of the Articles — not the real document."

"Oh, phew," Clementine said. She took her hand away from her mouth and looked relieved. "Still, even if it is just a copy, it's pretty rude."

"How'd they get the case open?" Amal asked, trying the lid. It was definitely locked.

"Hmm," Wilson said. "Good question." He squatted down beside the display and traced the slim crack where the lid met the body of the case, running his finger along it. "Maybe there's a way to pop the lock."

"Hey, you! What're you doing with that case?" a gruff voice called from behind them.

The four friends spun around. Standing in the doorway to the Hall of Documents was a huge man in a blue security uniform, and he did *not* look happy.

CHAPTER 3

Looking Guilty

"What are you kids up to?" the security guard asked angrily, stomping toward them.

Raining didn't recognize the guard, which was a little surprising. He spent so much time hanging around the museum that he knew almost everyone who worked there.

"We were just about to go find a security guard," Raining stammered. He and his friends all stepped quickly back from the display case housing the Articles of Confederation. "There's —"

But the big security man cut him off when he stared down into the case. "You little vandals," he said, snatching Raining and Wilson by their shirt collars. "You're all coming down to the security office with me — now!"

"But, sir!" Clementine protested. "We didn't do it! We just found it like this. And like Raining said, we were about to go get someone!"

"Exactly," Amal said. "In fact, Raining's dad works here. He's a big shot here — at least I think he is."

The guard sneered down at Raining. "Ah," he said, and a smile crawled to his face. "I know who you are. You're that Indian kid."

Raining's face got hot with anger. "My father and I are Ojibwe," he said tightly. "Indians live in India."

The guard ignored the correction. "I've heard you and your friends hang around the museum a lot," he growled. "I knew it wouldn't be long before I found the four of you getting into trouble."

"So you're new?" Raining asked. That would explain why he hadn't recognized the guard.

"Started last week," the guard snarled. "And no more questions. The four of you are coming with me."

With that, the man took Raining by the wrist and led him out of the Hall of Documents. Wilson, Clementine, and Amal all trailed after them. After all, what choice did they have?

CHAPTER 4
Troublemakers

A few moments later, Raining and his friends all stood side by side in the gleaming white security room in front of Ms. Garrison, the head of security. She looked back at them from behind her big desk.

"I caught these four kids writing graffiti on the Declaration of Independence," the guard said. He stood behind Raining, Wilson, Clementine, and Amal.

"These four, Mr. Poole?" Ms. Garrison said. She looked at the new guard as if she was quite confused. She probably was. "Are you sure it was *these* four?"

"Of course I'm sure," the security guard snapped. "Look here, Ms. Garrison. I've been a security guard for fifteen years, since the day I finished high school. Don't you think for a moment that I don't know how to do my job!"

"I'd never dream of suggesting such a thing, Mr. Poole," Ms. Garrison replied calmly. "I just want to make sure I have all the facts straight. So, to clarify, you saw *these* four children — four children whom I've known for a long time, three of them for most of their lives — open the case of the Declaration of Independence and scribble on it with a marker?"

Raining spoke up quietly. "It was the Articles of Confederation," he said.

Mr. Poole turned around and glared at Raining. "You, hush," he said. Then he looked back at Ms. Garrison. "Well, I didn't actually *see* them doing the scribbling. But they were *there*, and they're *kids*, and kids are usually up to no good."

Ms. Garrison raised an eyebrow at that. "Is that right?" she said.

Mr. Poole nodded vigorously. "Besides, this is Mr. Sam's kid. You know how those people feel about American history."

"*Those* people?" Ms. Garrison echoed.

"Indians!" Mr. Poole snapped impatiently.

Raining watched the security guard's mean eyes as they fell first on him, then on Amal. It looked like he was going to say something about her, too, when Ms. Garrison suddenly pushed back her chair and stood up.

"Mr. Poole," she said, leaning over her desk and looking the security guard right in the eye, "these four children are some of the smartest, most capable, most responsible, not to mention kindest, people I've ever known."

Raining felt his face go warm. Next to him, Clementine blushed, too.

"I assure you," Ms. Garrison went on, "they are not responsible for whatever crime was committed. I would vouch for these children in anything."

"But —" Mr. Poole protested.

"That's enough," Ms. Garrison silenced him. "You get back to your patrolling. I'll speak to these children for a minute."

Mr. Poole grunted and turned around to leave. He gave all four kids a long glare on his way out of the room. When the door closed behind him, Raining breathed a long sigh of relief.

"I'm sorry," Ms. Garrison said, shaking her head. She dropped into her seat and let her body sag a little. She looked exhausted. "You kids don't deserve that kind of treatment."

"It's all right," Raining said quietly.

"It most certainly is *not* all right," Ms. Garrison said. "That man is prejudiced and rude. He won't last long as a member of my security team if his attitude doesn't change, that's for sure."

Raining smiled a little at that. He'd known Ms. Garrison a long time and she'd never been anything but nice to him.

The head of security shook her head again. "It's such a shame, too," she said. "I was planning to find you kids today and ask you to look after Mr. Poole's son."

"He has a son?" Raining asked. "How old is he?"

Ms. Garrison looked them all over. "I think he's just about your age, Clementine," she said. "You're thirteen now, aren't you?"

Clementine smiled and nodded. She was tall for her age, and a lot of the time, most grown-ups guessed she was older because of that. It was nice that Ms. Garrison cared and listened enough to know the right number.

"Well, his name is Kenny," Ms. Garrison continued, "and he's around here someplace. I saw him this morning wandering through the courtyard. He looked downright miserable."

"Why?" Amal said. "Because that jerk is his dad?"

Raining laughed, but Clementine elbowed Amal and shushed her.

"Because," Ms. Garrison said over the kids' snickering and bickering, "he misses his friends back in Miami."

"Ooh," Amal said. "He's from Miami? With beaches and ocean and surfing? Lucky."

"Perhaps," Ms. Garrison said, "but he left all of that — and all of his friends back home — when he moved to Capitol City. Surely you can imagine how that might feel."

Amal nodded. She knew exactly how that felt. She had only moved to Capitol City a few months before. Luckily she'd made new best friends in Raining, Wilson, and Clementine, but she'd been very sad at first.

"I sure can," Amal said. She nodded toward her friends. "If it wasn't for these three, I'd probably be pretty miserable too."

"We'll find him," Raining assured Ms. Garrison. "And we'll do our best to make him feel welcome."

"Right," said Amal, putting an arm around Raining. "Even if his dad is a total jerk."

Clementine elbowed her again, and Ms. Garrison smiled. "Out of my office, you troublemakers!" she said with a laugh.

CHAPTER 5
Special Guests

"Kenny Poole," Clementine said, shoving her hands into the pockets of her paint-splattered jeans. Nearly every piece of clothing she owned was paint-splattered, actually. It was part of Clementine's creative charm. "It has a nice ring to it, doesn't it?"

Amal laughed. "I think you just like the word 'pool,'" she pointed out.

Clementine shrugged. "It's summer," she said. "Of course I do."

"Where do you think he is?" Wilson asked. He stopped in front of the huge museum map in the lobby just outside Ms. Garrison's office.

"We might as well try the courtyard first," Amal said. She pointed to a big green square in the center of the map that represented the museum's outdoor space. "That's where Ms. Garrison saw him."

The four friends strolled slowly across the front gallery. Huge marble statues of famous Americans, all sitting astride great stone steeds and holding graceful swords high in the air, flanked the main walkway.

The group was in no hurry. Though they'd promised Ms. Garrison to be friendly to Kenny, they'd already met his father, and they didn't exactly get along with him.

The courtyard doors stood at the far end of the statuary where bright sunlight was streaming in. Light reflected off the fat leaves of the plants in the courtyard, tinting the big gallery in shades of white and green.

Just then, footsteps rang through the huge hall. Raining looked over his shoulder and found a group of men and women — all dressed in dark suits and walking with purpose and confidence. Leading them was Dr. Hilary Bass, the president of the museum and the foremost American historian in Capitol City.

"Good morning, Dr. Bass," Raining said as the group reached him and his friends.

"Oh, Raining, hello," said Dr. Bass. She turned to the group with her. "Why don't you all continue on to the courtyard?" she suggested. "I'll join you in just a moment."

"Are they some kind of special guests of the museum today?" Raining asked after the group had moved outside.

Dr. Bass nodded. "They came in from our sister city in China," she explained. "They'll be taking a tour of all of Capitol City's museums over the next few days."

"Wow, too bad they had to come today of all days," said Amal.

Dr. Bass looked taken aback. "What do you mean?" she asked. "The weather today is perfect. I'm sure our guests will enjoy the courtyard. In fact, I thought we might have our lunch outside."

"Not because of the weather," Wilson said. "She means because of the vandalism upstairs. You haven't heard?"

Dr. Bass gasped. "Vandalism?" she said.

"It's probably nothing," said Raining. He forced himself to smile like it was no big deal. "We just saw some teeny tiny graffiti marks in the Flag Room."

"And the Hall of Documents," Clementine added.

"Oh, my," said Dr. Bass, her hand still covering her mouth. "I'll have to keep our guests away from those exhibits until we get to the bottom of this. I wouldn't want them to think that sort of thing is acceptable here." With that, she wandered toward the courtyard.

Raining watched her go. "Well," he said, "I don't think Kenny's out there."

"I sure wouldn't stay out there if I were him," Amal said, crossing her arms. "If I was feeling down and that crew of fancy-pants showed up, I'd find somewhere else to mope ASAP."

"You know the museum better than any of us, Raining," Clementine said. "Where would you hide out?"

Raining didn't even have to think about it. If he really wanted to be by himself, there was only one place he'd go.

CHAPTER 6
The New Kid

"The Parade of Great Americans," Raining said a few minutes later as he led his friends to an out-of-the-way exhibit. He pulled open the double doors marked "Do Not Enter – Exhibit Closed!"

Beyond the doors, it was nearly pitch black. Raining knew his way around perfectly, though. He led his friends along the narrow, sloping center aisle. He let his hands run over the velvet seatbacks.

After fewer than fifty paces, Raining stopped and turned around. "Got a flashlight, Wilson?" he asked.

Wilson obliged. He almost always had a penlight with him, and today was no exception. Soon the theater they were standing in was ever so slightly brighter. Wilson swung the narrow beam of his little flashlight here and there, illuminating the stage, the curtain, and the seats.

Finally, he pointed the light toward the wings and found the famous Americans themselves. Wilson nearly dropped the flashlight in surprise as he caught sight of the frozen, lifelike faces staring back at them. Amal let out a clipped shriek.

Clementine gasped and covered her mouth.

Raining couldn't help laughing. "Don't worry, guys," he said. "They're not real." He grabbed Wilson's flashlight and climbed up onto the stage. Then he pointed at each of the stock-still faces in turn.

The first was a young woman with a wide smile and short, dark hair. "Sally Ride," Raining said.

"Ooh!" said Amal. "I know her!"

Raining smiled. Of course Amal knew who Sally Ride was — her father worked at the Air and Space Museum, and Sally Ride had been the first woman to go into space.

The next motionless face was a woman with a sharp chin and a strong nose. Her dark hair was parted down the middle and plaited into two long braids. "Sacagawea," Raining said.

His friends nodded in recognition. Sacagawea was an indigenous American who'd led a very difficult life, but had proved to be very important to two famous explorers: Meriwether Lewis and William Clark. The United States government had eventually honored Sacagawea for her achievements.

The next face was round and pleasant, but stern-looking with a thin mustache and wide-open mouth, like he was speaking to a crowd.

They all recognized him right away. "Doctor Martin Luther King Junior," Wilson said.

Raining nodded. "There are more backstage, if you guys want to see," he offered, handing the flashlight back to Wilson.

"No, thanks," Wilson said, shaking his head. "It's pretty creepy in here."

"Believe me," Raining said, "it's not as creepy as the show they used to put on in here. The statues would move across the stage and talk to the audience. My father took me a couple times before they shut it down for good."

"Why'd they shut it down?" Amal asked. She jumped up on stage to get a closer look at the statues.

Raining shrugged. "I think it just got too expensive to keep up. These things break down all the time."

"Hey, are we allowed in here?" Clementine asked. She leaned her palms on the stage floor as Raining hopped down. "I mean, since it's closed and everything."

"Ms. Garrison caught me in here once," Raining said. "She didn't seem to care. She just wants me to be careful and quiet."

"Well," said Amal, taking a seat on the edge of the stage. "I don't think Kenny Poole is here."

"What makes you say that?" a new voice from behind the statues asked. A boy stepped out of the darkness, slipping carefully between Sally Ride and Sacagawea.

"Who are you?" Amal asked, crossing her arms. "You shouldn't be back there."

"It's Kenny Poole," Clementine said. "Obviously."

Kenny looked a lot like his father — tall and broad, with a nose that might have been broken once or twice combined with a strong jaw and a sharp chin.

Raining thought he looked much older than thirteen, but then again, so did Clementine, so he decided to keep his mouth shut.

Kenny walked over to them and dropped down from the stage. When his feet hit the ground they seemed to shake the whole room. "You're not supposed to be in here either," he said. "If I go get my dad, he'll kick you all out of the museum for the rest of your lives. He'll probably even call the cops."

Amal gave him a doubtful look. "You're in here too," she snapped. "Don't you think he's going to wonder why?"

"I'll just tell him I came in here to catch you guys," Kenny said, shrugging. "He'll believe me."

Clementine clucked her tongue. "We only came in here to look for you," she said. "Ms. Garrison said you might need a friend today."

Kenny laughed. "Yeah, right," he said. "Like I'd want to be friends with two little kids, a girl with paint all over her, and *you*." As he finished talking, he spun to glare at Amal.

"What's that supposed to mean?" Amal said, putting her fists on her hips and glaring back at Kenny.

Kenny rubbed his nose with the back of his hand. "You're wearing a head scarf," he said. "I know what that means."

Amal was about to say something in reply when Clementine suddenly stepped forward.

"This was obviously a bad idea," Clementine said. "If you want to sit in the dark and be miserable and horrible by yourself, feel free." She turned to the others. "Come on, guys. We have a mystery to solve anyway."

Raining led the way back up the dark aisle and slowly opened the double doors to make sure the hall outside was still empty.

"Wait a second," Kenny called after them. "What mystery?"

Wilson hesitated for a moment but then said, "Someone's been writing graffiti in the museum."

"In black marker?" Kenny said. "Because I just found some backstage. Wanna see?"

CHAPTER 7
More Graffiti

"I don't think I want this junior gorilla investigating with us," Amal said. She didn't bother trying to whisper so Kenny wouldn't hear her.

"I know," Raining replied. He didn't really want him around either. It seemed like Kenny was every bit as mean and hateful as his father. "But he knows where the graffiti is, so what choice do we have?"

Reluctantly the four friends headed back down the aisle and followed Kenny backstage.

"See for yourselves," Kenny said, motioning to the wall behind the retired Great Americans. The words, "This musem sux n this country sux" were scrawled in messy black handwriting.

"Not very good spelling," Wilson pointed out.

Kenny shrugged. "Whatever. I found some more in the currency exhibit."

"The history of money," Amal said, rubbing her hands together. "I hope they hand out free samples there."

"I think you're out of luck," Clementine said with a laugh.

Raining, Wilson, Clementine, Amal, and Kenny all headed up to the Currency Hall on the second floor. On the way there, they passed by the group of Chinese visitors again as Dr. Bass led them down the big main stairs.

"I don't know what we were expecting," one of the men was saying. He wore a dark gray suit, and his face was red with anger — and exertion from walking all over the museum. "We should have known Americans would know nothing about hospitality."

"Please, Mr. Wu," Dr. Bass pleaded. "You can hardly blame the museum that your newspaper blew away!"

"And my wife's coffee had cream in it!" Mr. Wu shouted. "She is lactose intolerant!"

"We didn't know," Dr. Bass said as she hurried down the stairs beside the angry Mr. Wu.

The kids quickly stepped out of the way as the big group passed. Dr. Bass tried to smile at Raining and his friends, but it was no use. She was obviously having a very bad day.

"I guess they're not very happy," Raining said.

"Mmhm," said Amal. "And it seems like Mr. Wu doesn't like the United States very much."

She shot a pointed glance at Raining, and he knew just what it meant — Mr.

Wu might be their best suspect yet. After all, didn't the graffiti backstage say "this country sux"?

* * *

"That is the biggest coin I've ever seen," Wilson said as they stepped into the Currency Hall.

He was certainly right. Hanging on the rear wall of the hall was a huge silver coin featuring an image of Walking Liberty — the Statue of Liberty walking in front of a huge shining sunrise.

"It's not real, silly," Clementine said with a grin. She strode clear across the hall. "But it is beautiful, isn't it?"

"And popular," Raining pointed out. "In fact, that image has appeared on two coins — a half dollar and a pure silver dollar coin."

The Currency Hall displayed bills and coins from throughout the history of the United States. There was even currency from before that, when each colony had used its own crazy-looking money.

Some of the bills and coins were copies, like the Walking Liberty image, but some of the examples were actual currency that was old enough to be obsolete or had been taken out of circulation just for the museum.

"How much you think this room is worth?" Kenny asked, leaning over a case of bills with face values of as little as two dollars and as much as one hundred thousand dollars.

Amal stepped up next to him. "Why?" she asked. "Planning on stealing it?"

"Maybe," Kenny said, smirking. "I'll blame it on you nerds."

"Very funny," Raining said sarcastically. "I think people would notice if you suddenly had a million bucks in retired bills in your pocket."

"Yeah," Amal said. "Even your dad would have to admit you were guilty."

Kenny shrugged. "Maybe," he said. Then he walked away from the case to the map in the middle of the room. "Here's where I saw the graffiti."

The four friends followed after him and stood in a half circle in front of the map. It was a funny-looking drawing. Though it was obviously shaped like the United

States, it didn't have any state borders or any words on it. Instead it was covered with a confusing web of thin red lines — it was almost as if someone had taken a straight-edge ruler and a pen and gone crazy.

"That's not graffiti," Raining said. "The lines show the movement of a single one-dollar bill across the country."

"Wow," said Wilson. He stood on tiptoes and leaned close to the map. "It went from Florida to Oregon in one step! That's amazing."

"So it got on a plane," Kenny said, rolling his eyes. "Big whoop. And that's not the graffiti I meant. How dumb do you think I am?"

Amal started to open her mouth.

"Don't answer that," Kenny said, cutting her off. "Anyway, the graffiti is over here." He stepped around behind the map and pointed out some black marker scribbled on the back. This time the graffiti said, "I HATE THIS PLACE."

"Another one about how awful it is here," Amal said, shaking her head. "It has to be Mr. Wu."

"I don't think so," said Kenny. "Mr. Wu isn't the only person around here who hates this country."

"Who else does?" Clementine asked.

"She does," Kenny said. He glared at Amal. "Everyone knows people like you hate this country."

"People like me?" Amal said.

Raining could tell she was getting very angry, and he didn't blame her. Kenny was way out of line.

"Yup," said Kenny. "And people like him, too." He nodded toward Raining. "And probably him." This time he pointed at Wilson.

Clementine looked furious. "Forget this jerk," she said. "Nice name or not, he's a bad guy. Let's go."

The four friends left Kenny behind in the Currency Hall.

"Good luck with your mystery!" Kenny called after them, laughing snidely as they walked out of the room. "Nerds!"

They stepped into the corridor. Amal looked mad enough to spit.

"Don't let him bother you," Wilson said, taking Amal's hand. "He's trying to make you mad."

"Well, it's working!" Amal said, looking angry and upset.

"I know," Clementine said. "But he's a jerk. Don't give him the satisfaction."

Just then, a girl stepped up to them. "Who are you guys talking about?" the girl snapped.

"Ruthie Rothchild," Clementine said under her breath. "Great. Just who I wanted to run into." She was being sarcastic, of course. None of the four friends liked Ruthie at all, but Clementine probably disliked her the most.

"Oh, come on," Ruthie said, smirking. "I just want to know who my new best friend is. After all, anyone who's got the four of you looking so angry is bound to be my favorite person."

"You're hilarious," Amal snapped. She rolled her eyes, then grabbed Clementine's elbow and shoved past Ruthie. The boys followed quickly after them.

"Are you thinking what I'm thinking?" Wilson asked when they were out of earshot.

Clementine nodded vigorously. "Rude, nasty comments scrawled all over the building?" she said. "Sounds like Ruthie Rothchild to me!"

CHAPTER 8
The Suspects

"Okay, so here's what we know so far," Raining said a few minutes later. They all sat together in the corner of the cafeteria. "Someone is vandalizing the museum. Whoever it is might hate the United States."

As they ate a quick lunch, Raining pulled out his notepad. He scribbled down two names: Mr. Wu and Ruthie Rothchild.

"Just two suspects," Amal said.

"Well . . ." said Clementine. She let her voice trail off.

"Well, what?" Raining asked.

Clementine looked down at her hands. "I didn't want to say this before," she said, "but Kenny and his dad both suggested that there are a couple of other suspects."

"Who?" said Amal, leaning back in her chair.

Clementine didn't answer. She just stared down at her hands silently, seeming embarrassed to have even brought it up.

"I know who she means," Wilson said, sounding angry. "And it's ridiculous."

Clementine finally looked up. "I know it is," she said. "Believe me, I do. But we have to eliminate every possibility. If we don't, you know Kenny and his dad will bring it up."

"Wait a second," said Raining. His heart seemed to thump a little harder in his chest. "I still don't know who the other two suspects are."

"She means you and Amal," Wilson said. His stare at Clementine was as icy as the cafeteria slushies.

Raining's skin felt icy too. "Do you?" he asked.

Clementine looked at him pleadingly. "*I* don't think that," she insisted. "I really don't. I just meant that Kenny and his dad both brought it up. And if they did, someone else might too. We have to be thorough."

"Not *that* thorough," Amal said. "You know that Raining and I would never do anything like that."

Clementine looked down again. "I know," she said. "I'm sorry. I shouldn't have brought it up."

No one spoke for a few minutes. Finally Raining pushed back his chair and stood up. "We should get back to work," he said, breaking the awkward silence that had fallen over the group. "The vandal might be scribbling mustaches on the presidential portraits by now."

Amal chuckled, just as he'd meant her to, and Wilson stood up to clear their trays.

Clementine stood up too. "Guys, I'm really sorry," she said again. "I —"

"Do you think one of us did it?" Amal interrupted.

Clementine shook her head. "Of course not."

"Then let's just move on," Amal said. "For starters, maybe you can get a look in Ruthie's bag."

"What for?" Clementine asked as the four of them headed for the cafeteria doors.

"That's easy," Raining said. "To see if she has a black marker in there, of course."

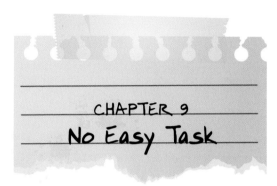

CHAPTER 9
No Easy Task

Despite what Raining had said, their task was anything *but* easy. First they had to find Ruthie. That part wasn't so hard. They eventually spotted her in the courtyard eating a Popsicle.

The good news was she had her bag with her. The bad news? She was using it as a pillow as she lay on her back, soaking up the sun.

"How am I supposed to get a look in there?" Clementine whispered.

The four friends hunched together behind one of the fat little palm trees that decorated the courtyard and kept an eye on their arch-nemesis.

"Maybe she's asleep," Amal suggested hopefully.

"With a Popsicle in her mouth?" said Raining. "I don't think so. That's impossible. Or at least I think it is."

"You'll have to trick her," Amal said. "Get her to sit up."

"Fine," Clementine said as she stepped out from behind their tree. "I'll get her to sit up, *you* grab the bag."

"Ugh," Amal said, making a face. "Fine."

"What about us?" Raining asked. "What are we supposed to do?"

"You two wait here," Amal said. "Keep an eye out for trouble."

"Trouble?" said Wilson. "What kind of trouble?"

"Like Kenny Poole," Amal said. "Or his dad."

With that, Clementine and Amal were off. As the boys watched, they strolled over to where Ruthie was lounging. When she spotted them approaching, Ruthie sat up and took off her sunglasses. She said something to Clementine and then to Amal. Amal said something back.

Clementine took a seat on the bench next to Ruthie, and almost immediately, Ruthie slid all the way to the other end.

Clementine was now between Ruthie and Ruthie's bag.

As Raining watched, Clementine inched closer to the bag until — *whoops!* The bag fell off the end of the bench and plopped onto the red-brick walkway, spilling its contents all over the path.

"You idiot!" Ruthie shouted, jumping to her feet as Amal and Clementine hurried to scoop up the spilled items.

Ruthie knocked them out of the way. "I'll get it," she shouted. "Just get away from me."

Clementine looked up from the mess of junk on the bricks and glanced over at the boys. She shook her head and shrugged.

"I guess she doesn't have a black marker in there," Raining said.

"That leaves Mr. Wu," said Wilson.

Both boys stood up straight as the girls headed back toward them. Suddenly Amal and Clementine stopped, looking startled. At the same moment, a heavy hand grabbed Raining's shoulder.

"Well, well, well," a stern voice said from behind him. Raining turned around to see Mr. Poole, the security guard, glaring down at him. "Looks like the two little thugs are making trouble again."

CHAPTER 10
The Real Culprit

"We're not doing anything!" Raining protested.

"Yeah," said Amal as she and Clementine ran up to the group. "They were just standing there."

"Oh, yeah?" said Mr. Poole. "Then what's that?" He pointed at some black scribbles on a nearby tree trunk.

"I don't know! I didn't even see that!" Raining said.

"What does it even say?" Clementine asked, leaning over.

Amal leaned over too. "'This courtyard stinks,'" she read aloud.

"All right," Mr. Poole said. "Back to Garrison's office. This time she'll have to take action."

"But it wasn't us!" Raining insisted, trying to pull away.

"Oh, really? Then who was it?" Poole said. "You two were skulking by this tree. Besides, I spoke to Kenny, and he tells me he found some other nasty notes and that you four were hanging around in those places, too."

"That's a lie!" Clementine said. "Kenny is the one who showed us that graffiti. That's the only reason we were anywhere near it!"

Raining struggled against Mr. Poole's strong grip, but it was no use. The guard wasn't letting go.

Wilson leaned close and whispered, "We only have one suspect left."

"So?" Raining said. "What's your point?"

"We have to get to Mr. Wu so we can follow up," Wilson said. "We don't have time to get held up at Ms. Garrison's office again."

Raining squirmed and twisted some more, but the big guard's grip was too strong.

"Quit struggling," Mr. Poole snarled.

Wilson smiled and lifted his foot. Then he brought it down — hard — on Mr. Poole's foot.

"Yow!" Mr. Poole shouted. He let go of Raining so he could grab his hurt foot with both hands, which made him hop around on the other foot. After a few hops, the security guard lost his balance and tumbled backward into the hydrangea bush.

"Let's go!" Wilson said.

Amal laughed and grabbed Raining's hand, and they followed after Wilson toward the courtyard's back exit.

"You guys!" Clementine called, still standing over the fallen guard. "He might be hurt!"

"He's fine!" Wilson assured her, holding open the big glass door at the far end of the courtyard. "Hurry up before he grabs you!"

Clementine hesitated for another moment, glancing back and forth between her friends and the security guard. But finally she turned and followed them inside, into the darkness of the Hall of American Artists — her favorite part of the museum.

"We have to find Mr. Wu quickly, or Poole will grab us again for sure," Amal said. "Everyone, think. If you were a group of important visitors, where would you go?"

"Maybe they're eating lunch," Raining suggested. He and his friends had already eaten, but they were often the first people in line at the cafeteria. Maybe the grown-ups, especially a group of important, visiting growno-ups, were a bit more restrained.

"Nope," Clementine said, shaking her head. "Remember Dr. Bass said they were going to have lunch in the courtyard. We were just there. No Mr. Wu."

Raining nodded. "You're right, I forgot she said that."

Just then, Dr. Bass came strolling through the gallery. She looked miserable.

"Everything okay, Dr. Bass?" Clementine said.

The doctor flinched. She hadn't even noticed the kids were there. "Oh, hello," she said. "Sorry, I'm a little distracted."

"Where are your guests?" Raining asked.

The doctor frowned at them. "That's just why I'm so distracted," she said. "They left."

"Left?" Raining said. "I thought they were special guests from our sister city in China. Why would they leave?"

"And before lunch!" Amal said.

"Apparently," Dr. Bass said, clearly irritated, "our hospitality wasn't to their liking."

"Oh, no! What happened?" asked Wilson.

"Oh, who knows," Dr. Bass said. She dropped sullenly onto a bench set next to a painting by Norman Rockwell. "I think the whole bunch of them were offended by yet another piece of graffiti."

"They were offended by it?" Wilson said. "Huh."

"What do you mean 'huh'?" Dr. Bass said, looking up.

"Well, we thought Mr. Wu might be the vandal," Raining admitted. "We were coming to find you so we could confront him about it."

"Oh, no," Dr. Bass said. She smoothed the front of her pants and stood up. "There's no way Mr. Wu is responsible. He was deeply troubled by the whole thing. He said it showed that we Americans have no respect for our own vast and impressive culture and education system. Whatever that means."

"So if it wasn't Mr. Wu," Clementine said, "and it wasn't silly old Ruthie Rothchild —"

"And it clearly wasn't one of us," Amal added quickly.

Clementine nodded. "Then who was it?"

Just then, Dr. Bass gasped. "Look at *that*!" she said, pointing behind them.

The kids turned around to see a jumble of crazy-looking letters scrawled on one of the big glass doors leading to the courtyard.

"I can't figure out what it says," Raining said.

The girls screwed up their faces as they tried to decipher the odd black writing. It made no sense.

Suddenly Wilson had an idea. He hurried over and swung open the door. He stepped into the courtyard and let the door swing shut again behind him. Then he looked at the letters from the other side and smiled.

"They were written from this side!" Wilson called to his friends and Dr. Bass. "They say, 'Ms. Garrison is a stinker.' Wow."

"That's not very nice," Dr. Bass said. She stomped toward the door, pulled it open, and rubbed a couple of letters with her thumb. The ink smeared under her touch. "It's fresh," she said. "Not even dry yet."

"That cinches it, then," Raining said as he and the girls joined Dr. Bass and Wilson

near the door. "It definitely couldn't have been Mr. Wu."

"That's right," Dr. Bass agreed. "He's been gone for ages. If it were him, the marker wouldn't still be wet."

Raining looked out into the courtyard at the tree he and Wilson had hid behind earlier. Mr. Poole wasn't there anymore, but he remembered the graffiti that had been there. He remembered the graffiti that had been backstage. He remembered the graffiti from the Currency Hall, and the Flag Room, and the Hall of Documents.

Then he remembered the one other person he'd met today who hated this museum as much as Mr. Wu seemed to hate this country — and had had plenty of opportunity to be in every single one of those places.

"Guys," Raining said as he recognized a big, glum-looking boy sitting on the same bench Ruthie had occupied earlier. "I think I know who our vandal is — Kenny Poole."

CHAPTER 11
An Apology

The four sleuths and Dr. Bass tracked down Ms. Garrison and told her what they'd uncovered. Then they all went to find Mr. Poole. Raining explained everything to him.

No one was surprised that Poole didn't quite believe them.

"That's absurd," Mr. Poole said, but his face fell. "Kenny knows how important my job is here. Why, it's the first decent job I've had in years. We'd have to go back to Miami and live with my brother if I lost this job. Kenny knows that."

Raining nodded. "I think that's part of his plan, Mr. Poole," he said. "Kenny hates it here."

"Exactly," said Amal. "He wants to go back. I felt the same way right after *my* dad dragged me here from New York when he got a job at the Air and Space Museum down the road."

Mr. Poole's face went pale. He found a seat and ran his hand through his hair, looking upset and exhausted. "Why didn't he tell me?" he said.

"Would it have mattered?" Raining asked. "Would you have left the job and

Capitol City to go back to your brother's in Miami?"

Mr. Poole's mouth twisted, and his eyes fell. He shook his head. "No, I suppose not," he said.

"I think you'd better talk to Kenny," Ms. Garrison said, putting a hand on Mr. Poole's shoulder. "The museum can forgive this — no damage to any valuable exhibits has been done. We'll work something out."

"Work something out?" Mr. Poole said, looking up at his boss.

"Kenny will do some cleaning up," Dr. Bass said. "Maybe he can volunteer to help out with one of the lower-grade field trips."

"Amal and I volunteer for those all the time," Clementine offered with a smile. "It's a lot of fun."

"Yeah," Amal agreed. "We'll show him the ropes."

Mr. Poole smiled at the girls. "You're awfully nice considering how rude my boy and I have been to you today," he said. "I owe you all a big apology. And so does Kenny."

"We'll forgive you," Amal said. "Right, Raining?"

Raining thought about it for a long moment. There was a lot to forgive. But finally, he nodded. "Okay," he agreed. "You promise to be more open-minded to people you've never met, and all is forgiven."

Mr. Poole put his hand over his chest. "I promise," he said. "And Kenny will too. I suppose I'd better find him."

"He's in the courtyard," Raining said. "I think he'd probably like to talk to you."

Mr. Poole turned and strode toward the courtyard doors. But after a few steps, he stopped and turned back toward the four friends. "Thanks, kids. The museum — and my boy — have some great friends in you four."

Steve B.

About the Author

Steve Brezenoff is the author of more than fifty middle-grade chapter books, including the Field Trip Mysteries series, the Ravens Pass series of thrillers, and the Return to Titanic series. In his spare time, he enjoys video games, cycling, and cooking. Steve lives in Minneapolis with his wife, Beth, and their son and daughter.

Lisa W.

About the Illustrator

Lisa K. Weber is an illustrator currently living in Oakland, California. She graduated from Parsons School of Design in 2000 and then began freelancing. Since then, she has completed many print, animation, and design projects, including graphic novelizations of classic literature, character and background designs for children's cartoons, and textiles for dog clothing.

GLOSSARY

decipher (di-SYE-fur) — to figure out what something says, usually something that is badly written or hard to read

exhibit (eg-ZIB-it) — a public display or show

graffiti (gruh-FEE-tee) — illegal drawings or words people make on objects

indigenous (in-DIJ-uh-nuhs) — originally being from a particular place

juvenile (JOO-vuh-nuhl) — childish and immature

mar (MAHR) — to damage or make less perfect

prejudiced (PREJ-uh-dist) — to have fixed, negative opinions about a group of people

sleuth (SLOOTH) — someone who solves mysteries or is good at finding out facts

suspect (SUHS-pekt) — a person that is believed to have done something wrong

vandal (VAN-duhl) — a person that purposefully destroys or damages another person's things

DISCUSSION QUESTIONS

1. Kenny was pretty miserable after moving from Miami to Capitol City. Have you ever moved? Talk about how you felt when you got to your new home.

2. What is your favorite period of American history? Talk about your reasons.

3. Kenny and his dad made some very mean judgments about the four friends before knowing anything about them. Has someone ever judged you based only on how you looked? Talk about it.

WRITING PROMPTS

1. There have been many American flags throughout history — both official and unofficial. Design your own flag for the United States. Describe how it would look and explain your choices.

2. The four friends forgave Mr. Poole, even though what he said was very hurtful. Write about a time when you forgave someone, even though it wasn't easy.

3. Write a story about Kenny after he's been caught. Does he become friends with Raining, Amal, Wilson, and Clementine? Does he start to like living in Capitol City?

AMERICAN HISTORY INFORMATION

The National Museum of American History, which opened in Washington, D.C. in 1964, is home to more than three million artifacts important to America's history, including the original Star-Spangled Banner. The museum welcomes more than four million people each year. It is focused on helping visitors learn about America and its unique population.

Flag Facts:

The original Star-Spangled Banner was made in 1813 by flagmaker Mary Pickersgill and was 30 feet by 42 feet, or about one-fourth of a modern basketball court.

On September 14, 1814, Francis Scott Key wrote a poem about the Star-Spangled Banner flying over Fort McHenry after it survived a British attack. The poem was set to music and became a very popular patriotic song. In 1931, "The Star-Spangled Banner" officially became the national anthem of the United States.

American Documents Facts:

The Articles of Confederation were first put into use on November 15, 1777. They were later approved by all the thirteen states on March 1, 1781. The Articles gave most decision-making power to individual states.

A Constitutional Convention was held in Philadelphia, Pennsylvania from May 25 to September 17, 1787 to edit the Articles of Confederation. However, the committee of men ended up creating an entirely new document: **the United States Constitution**.

In 1789, the U.S. Constitution officially replaced the Articles of Confederation. The Constitution created three separate branches of government so that one person would never have too much power. The three branches are:

- Legislative — makes laws

- Executive — carries out laws

- Judicial — reviews laws

In addition to their own unique jobs, the branches aso work together to make sure the country runs smoothly and that the rights of citizens are not ignored.

Ready for more MYSTERY?

MUSEUM MYSTERIES

Check out all the Capitol City sleuths' adventures and help them solve crime in some of the city's most important museums!